The Truck Book

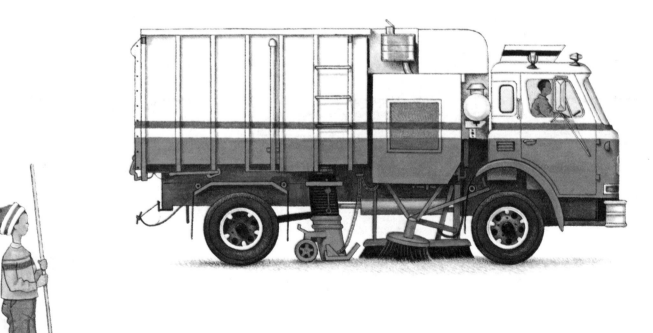

A Random House PICTUREBACK®

HARRY McNAUGHT

TRUCK
LOADING

RANDOM HOUSE 🏠 NEW YORK

EARLY ELECTRIC TRUCK

MODEL T FIRE ENGINE (1919)

MODEL T TRUCK (1921)

FIFTH AVENUE BUS, NEW YORK CITY (1907)

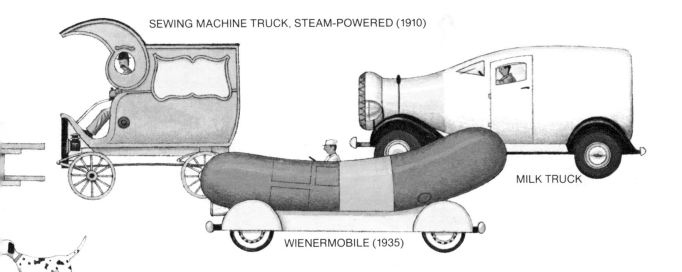

SEWING MACHINE TRUCK, STEAM-POWERED (1910)

WIENERMOBILE (1935)

MILK TRUCK

Trucks do important work. But they are fun to look at, too. Some of the early trucks were especially fun to see. One milk truck looked like a giant milk bottle. Its shape told people what kind of work it did.

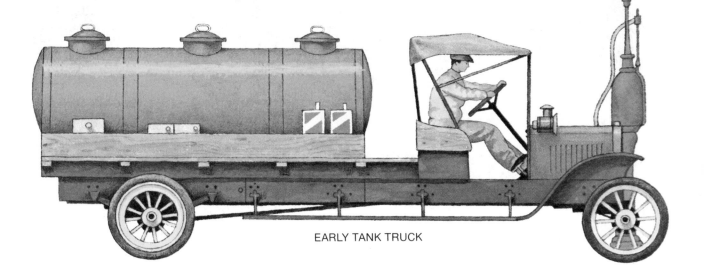

EARLY TANK TRUCK

Trucks go everywhere and do all kinds of work. They
help people clean the streets and put out fires.

Most trucks are built to carry heavy loads. Some are so big that they can even carry other trucks.

Some trucks can go where there are no paved roads. An off-highway dump truck travels on dirt roads or rough fields.

This one can carry 85 tons of rock. That is as much as 17 elephants weigh!

Specially built trucks are needed to lift
and move heavy things. The back of
a dump truck tilts to let its load slide out.

Cranes have a long arm called a boom that can lift heavy loads. A fork-lift truck has weights at the back so it can pick up heavy things without tipping over.

Trucks move tons of earth to make a new road.
A backhoe digs, lifts, and dumps loads of dirt. A tractor
hauls the dirt away. A grader makes the roadbed smooth by
dragging a blade along the ground. Other trucks help by
filling holes and smoothing out bumps.

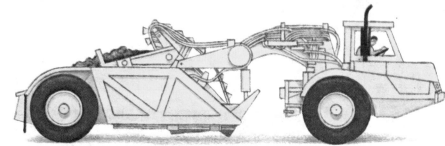

ELEVATING SCRAPER

GRADER

PAYLOADER

SANITATION TRUCK

Trucks come in all shapes and sizes. Big sanitation trucks haul garbage away. Huge moving vans can carry enough furniture to fill a house. People selling hot dogs push small hand trucks along the street.

HAND TRUCK

VENDOR'S TRUCK

TANK TRUCK

MOVING VAN

TRACTOR WITH TILT CAB

In the forest, logging trucks can quickly do jobs that once took lumberjacks many days of work. A log feller grabs a tree with its long arm. In just a few seconds, its powerful blades cut right through the tree trunk.

After the trees have been cut down, a grapple skidder gathers them up with its claw. Then it drags them to the loading area.

A log loader picks up logs and stacks them on a truck. A big tractor-trailer carries the logs to the lumber mill, where they will be cut into boards.

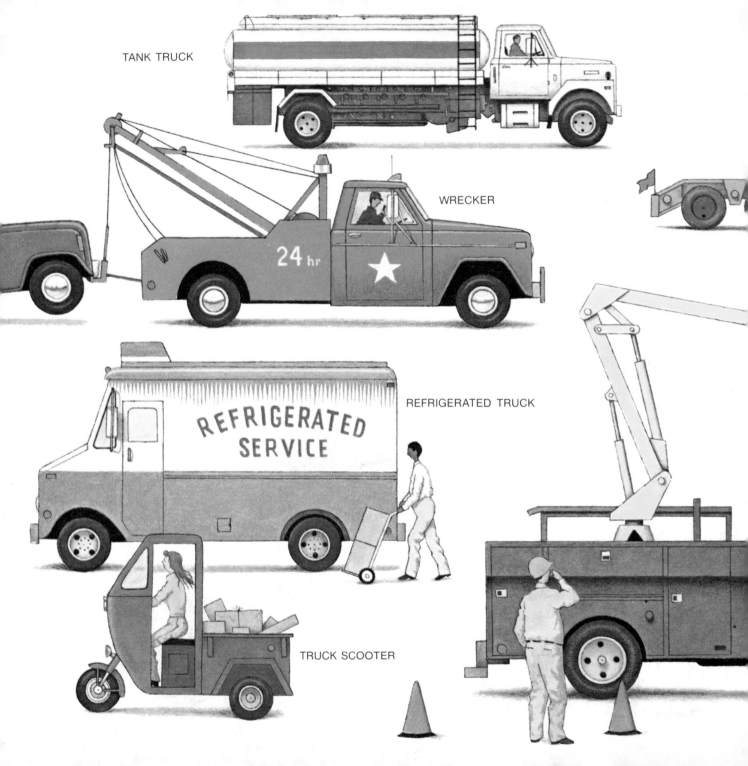

TANK TRUCK

WRECKER

24 hr

REFRIGERATED TRUCK

REFRIGERATED SERVICE

TRUCK SCOOTER

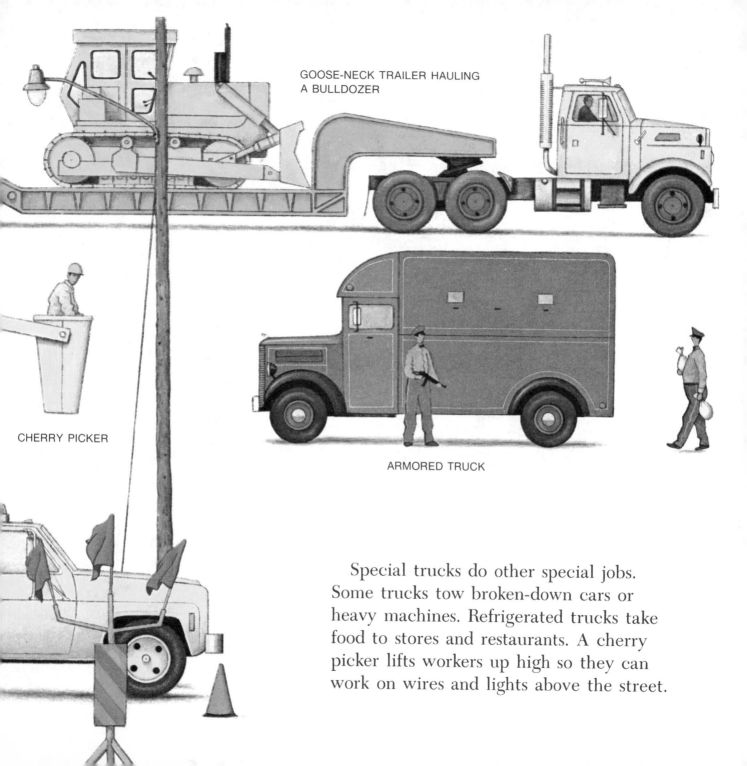

GOOSE-NECK TRAILER HAULING
A BULLDOZER

CHERRY PICKER

ARMORED TRUCK

Special trucks do other special jobs.
Some trucks tow broken-down cars or
heavy machines. Refrigerated trucks take
food to stores and restaurants. A cherry
picker lifts workers up high so they can
work on wires and lights above the street.

VOLKSWAGEN CAMPER

TRAILER HOME

There are trucks built for people to live in—
at least when they go on vacation! They drive
from place to place and stop off at campgrounds.
At night they sleep inside their camper trucks. Some small
trailers have tents attached to them. Other campers are
vans. Their roofs lift up so that people can walk around inside.
Most big motor homes have their own bathroom and kitchen.

TENT TRAILER

VAN CAMPER

PICKUP CAMPER

OFFICE

MOTOR HOME

When the fire station is quiet, fire fighters clean the trucks and check on ladders and hoses. Then, when there is a fire, the trucks are ready to go.

Sirens scream, bells ring, and lights flash, telling people on the street to move out of the way.

The hook-and-ladder truck helps fire fighters reach the top floors of tall buildings. The pumper sends water through the hoses to put out the fire.

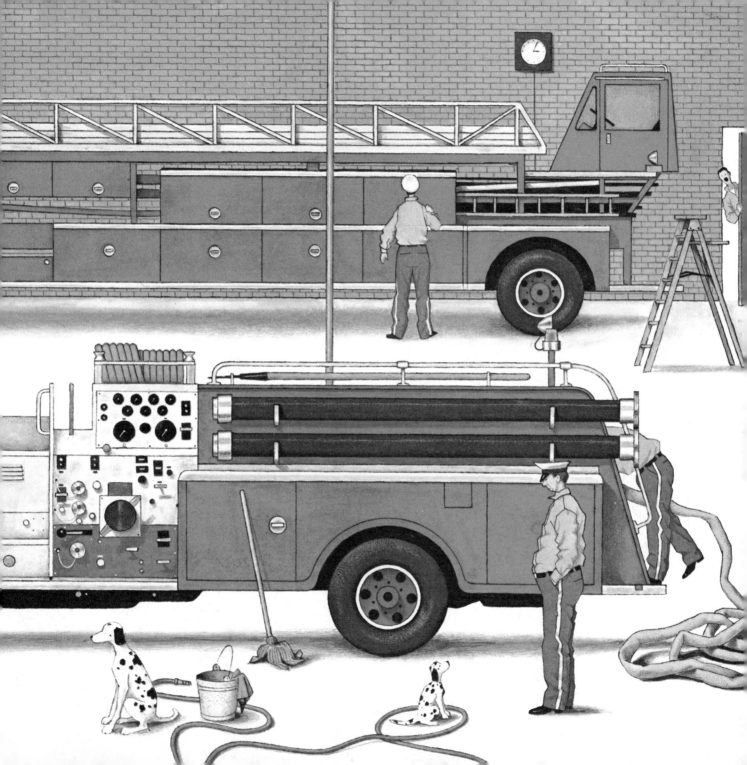

A new building is going up! Cranes lift
beams and pipes, batches of concrete,
and sections of walls to the top floors of
the new building.

This truck mixes water, clay, limestone, and gravel to make concrete. The concrete comes out of a chute at the back of the truck. Concrete is used to make sidewalks, floors, and foundations for buildings.

Buses carry people to stores, schools, offices, and factories. Some cities, like London and New York, have double-decker buses. It's fun to ride upstairs! Yellow school buses have special signal lights that go on whenever the bus stops. These lights tell other drivers to stop until the children have crossed the street safely.

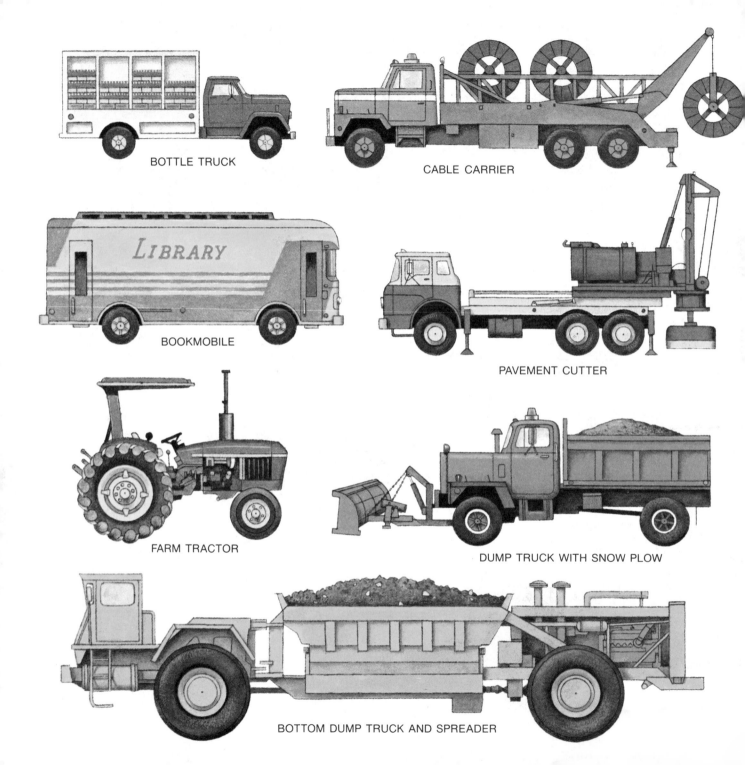

BOTTLE TRUCK

CABLE CARRIER

BOOKMOBILE

PAVEMENT CUTTER

FARM TRACTOR

DUMP TRUCK WITH SNOW PLOW

BOTTOM DUMP TRUCK AND SPREADER

TRACTOR-TRAILER WITH CAB UNDERNEATH

Trucks carry books. Trucks carry bottles. Trucks cut holes in city streets so workers can fix things underground. Some trucks dig holes in the ground and put telephone poles in place. Other trucks help repair holes in the road. Tractors pull plows in farm fields. Special trucks drive on railroad tracks.

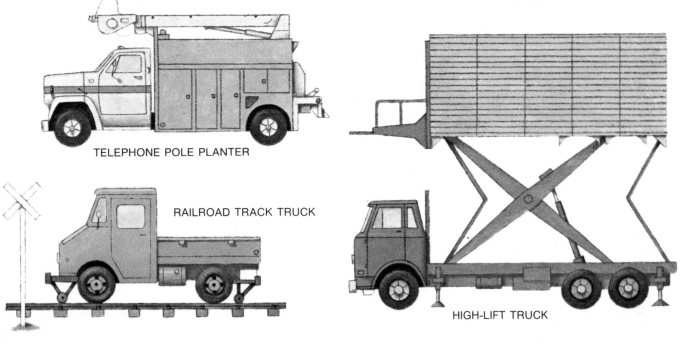

GLAZIER'S TRUCK

TELEPHONE POLE PLANTER

RAILROAD TRACK TRUCK

HIGH-LIFT TRUCK

Everywhere you go, trucks are hard at work.
And they are fun to look at.

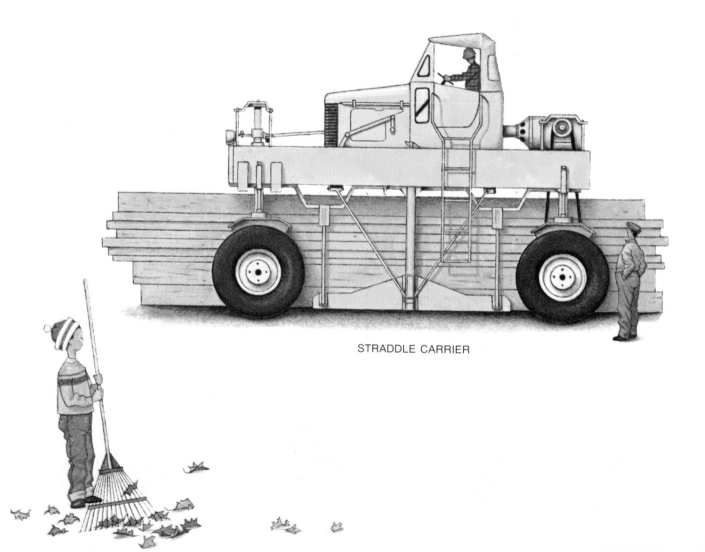

STRADDLE CARRIER